MR. IMPO[illegible]

and the Easter Egg Hu[illegible]

Roger Hargreaves

Original concept by
Roger Hargreaves

Written and illustrated by
Adam Hargreaves

EGMONT

Mr Happy lives in Happyland.

The happiest place in the World.

Where even the donkeys are happy.

Mr Happy lives in a house beside a lake and not long ago, just before Easter in fact, he decided to have a picnic for all his friends.

An Easter picnic on the shores of the lake.

And to make the day special he wanted to organize an Easter egg hunt.

Although not an Easter egg hunt like the previous year when Mr Lazy had hidden the eggs.

Being the lazy fellow he is, he had not hidden the eggs very well.

No, not at all well!

Mr Happy wanted someone who could hide the eggs better than anyone else.

And then he thought of Mr Impossible.

Mr Impossible as you might imagine can do the impossible.

The perfect person to hide Easter eggs!

And so Mr Impossible hid the eggs in impossible hiding places.

Places you would never think of.

Mr Happy went to bed a happy man.

But in the middle of the night Mr Happy awoke with a terrible thought.

What if nobody could find the Easter eggs?

But it was too late to do anything about it, the picnic was the next day.

All his friends arrived the next morning and a worried Mr Happy worried that his Easter egg hunt was going to be a disaster.

Would any eggs be found?

At first it seemed as though the Easter eggs were going to be impossible to find. But then Mr Bump found the first one.

He was so busy looking on the ground that he bumped into a tree knocking down an egg hidden high in the branches.

It fell on his head!

Mr Impossible had hidden one egg down
a rabbit hole.

Mr Tickle's long arm found that one.

There was a tiny egg hidden in the petals of a flower.

Mr Small found that one.

Mr Bounce found the one hidden behind the chimney pot.

Mr Strong found one hidden underneath a barn.

And Mr Tall found an Easter egg hidden, impossibly, in a cloud!

"Well done!" cried Mr Happy. "I think you have found all the Easter eggs."

"Not quite," said Mr Impossible. "There is one more to find and I bet nobody can find it. It's invisible!"

"That's impossible!" cried everyone in unison.

"Eggsactly!" chuckled Mr Impossible.

And then a voice piped up,

"I've found it!"

A voice seemingly out of nowhere.

But not nowhere, it was nobody.

Mr Nobody.

"Well," said Mr Happy. "You were right
Mr Impossible..."

"... Nobody did find it!"